Sir Pigglesworth's
Adventures in Cozumel

BOOK
6

By JoAnn Wagner and Sara Dean
Illustrations by David Darchicourt

Sir Pigglesworth Publishing, Inc.
1515 N. Town East Blvd, Suite 138-118
Mesquite, TX 5150

Revised October 2016
Printed in China
10 9 8 7 6 5 4 3 2

Paperback: ISBN 978-1-68055-087-0
Hardcover: ISBN 978-1-68055-088-7
EBook: ISBN 978-1-68055-089-4

To the charming citizens of Cozumel, Mexico…thank you for your kindness, your generous hospitality and your animated personalities! I met so many happy people who shared their smiles with me and encouraged me in my journey. Thank you for showing me your beautiful country!

To the amazing Captain and crew of the Carnival Breeze…I love how you accepted Sir Pigglesworth into your hearts and onto your ship. Thank you for your gracious hospitality and the many gifts you gave me! Bon Voyage...Happy Sailing!

JoAnn Wagner
July 2016

Olé - Viva Cozumel

Join our hoofed hero and his friends as they travel to Cozumel, Mexico. There Sir Pigglesworth learns about the local folklore, explores ancient ruins and flirts with pretty senoritas!!

The lovable master of mischief and mayhem takes a cruise with Princess Serena to help his friend JoAnn celebrate her birthday. The young piglet remembers how much fun he had on the last cruise he took to Bermuda with his friends and he can't wait to experience sailing on the Carnival Breeze...after all, it is the FUN ship!!

As soon as he steps on board and is welcomed by Captain Alcaras, he is ready to party. Because of his antics, it isn't long before every passenger knows the name Sir Pigglesworth...not always in a good way! And that's only on the ship. Come join our energetic rascal as he races around Cozumel with his friends trying to fit in as much fun as he can in a short time!

Get ready to learn and laugh,
and love "Sir Pigglesworth"
as he travels the world in
search of fun and adventure!

Sir Pigglesworth's
Adventures in Cozumel

Chapter 1

"I'm going to see JoAnn! I'm going to surprise her for her birthday!" Sir Pigglesworth was singing as he danced along the dock.

Everyone walking to the ship was watching him with a big smile. The little pig looked so happy!

His friend Princess Serena followed behind him holding her hands on his shoulders as she danced along with him.

Bill, who had arranged this surprise for JoAnn, smiled as he saw them coming.

He knew there was never a dull moment when their little pink friend was around!

"Hello, Bill!" Sir said happily as he finished his dance. Sir and Serena gave him a big hug!

They went up the gangplank into the lobby of the ship where Captain Vincenzo Alcaras was waiting to greet them.

"Hello," the captain said. "Welcome aboard the Carnival Breeze."

"Thank you," Serena said. Sir Pigglesworth was too excited to remember his manners. He bumped into Serena, knocking her into Bill who caught her just before she fell.

"I'm here to surprise JoAnn for her birthday! Do you know her? Everyone does! She writes books for kids. They're really funny! Have you seen her?"

Captain Alcaras laughed. "No, I haven't seen her, but she sounds interesting."

"Why don't you all join me for dinner as my birthday gift to her and you can introduce me."

Sir was so excited he jumped in the air throwing his hooves in all directions. He accidentally hit Serena again.

"That's it!" Serena mumbled under her breath. "I'm done being polite!"

Even though Sir Pigglesworth and Serena loved playing together, they fought like cats and dogs sometimes.

She lowered her head and started to charge at Sir like a bull, but Bill picked her up right before she reached him.

Ignoring Serena, Sir Pigglesworth turned to the lady beside him. "Have you ever taken a cruise?" he asked, not waiting for her answer.

"I have, and it is so much fun!" Sir started listing off all the things he did on his last cruise with his friends.

He got a faraway look in his eyes as he relived all of them in his mind. He'd had the best time ever!

He couldn't wait to see what adventures awaited him on this ship!

Chapter 2

After checking into their rooms, Sir Pigglesworth and Serena sneaked into JoAnn's cabin while Bill kept her busy on another part of the ship.

They wanted to surprise her. No surprise was complete in Sir Pigglesworth's eyes without jumping out and screaming "surprise!"

He couldn't wait to see JoAnn's face.

He knew she would be shocked to see both him and Serena.

Sir said he would hide under the bed. "I was going to hide under the bed!" Serena protested loudly.

She stomped her foot and made a face. Sir Pigglesworth crossed his hooves and pouted. It was a standoff!

They were still having a stare down when they heard Bill's voice just outside the cabin door.

They scrambled under the bed. There wasn't enough room for both of them.

When JoAnn and Bill opened the cabin door, they saw a pink curly tail and a pair of bright pink sandals sticking out from under the bed.

JoAnn squealed with delight. She knew right away that Sir had come to visit and brought a friend.

"You can come out now," Bill said, "We can see you."

"We can't!" cried Serena. "We're stuck here!"

Which was quickly followed by Sir Pigglesworth yelling, "Surprise!"

After Sir and Serena made it out from under the bed, JoAnn took them to sign up for Camp Ocean.

They joined the Stingray group for 5 year old kids.

It was a warm, sunny day so the group went outside on the deck. Spotting the children's pool right away, Serena and Sir raced over and jumped in.

They began to splash and see who could "piggy paddle" across the pool the fastest. Several kids joined in the fun.

Before long everyone raced up the stairs to a large orange winding slide and went sliding down.

The slide ended in the pool where everyone just missed landing on each other! They all laughed hysterically.

After swimming, Sir Pigglesworth couldn't seem to shake the water from his ears. He couldn't hear very well.

Every time he talked, he yelled.

"Bill!" he called loudly, even though he was only standing two feet from him.

"I want to buy JoAnn a birthday present. Will you take me to find something nice for her?"

"What did you have in mind?" Serena yelled back, because she had water in her ears, too.

"How about diamonds?" Sir asked.

Bill, who was getting a headache from all the yelling, quickly took them to the jewelry store.

The store manager greeted them. "Welcome to my store," he said.

"It's nice to meet you!" Sir shouted. "Do you have any diamonds?"

The manager took a step back and glanced at Bill. "He has water in his ears," Bill explained.

The manager laughed and led them to a glass case filled with sparkling diamond rings and earrings.

Sir wanted to buy them all, but he only had ten dollars. He couldn't afford to buy any of them.

He turned to Bill and shouted, "I guess you'll have to buy the diamonds for JoAnn. They're a little out of my price range."

"And by a little, he means a lot!" Princess Serena shouted.

Bill took them to the candy store. Sir Pigglesworth's eyes popped wide open when he saw all that candy!

His favorite chocolate bars were staring right at him.

The next time Bill and Serena saw him he was lying on the floor covered in candy wrappers and chocolate.

Bill cleaned up the mess while Sir Pigglesworth paid for his 'snack' and JoAnn's birthday present, which he had the clerk wrap in a fancy box with a big bow.

"It took all of my ten dollars," Sir told them as they walked out of the store, "but it was well worth it."

He burped and Serena playfully punched his arm.

"You little piggy," she laughed.

Chapter 3

Sir hid JoAnn's present in his cabin and took a nap until it was time for dinner.

JoAnn had mentioned they would be eating in the Sapphire Room. He couldn't wait to see the Sapphire jewels he was sure the room was made of!

When they walked in, he was surprised. He looked at the floor, the walls, the ceiling. Where were the sapphires?

He whispered this to Serena, who laughed. "You're silly," she said. "The food is made of sapphires, not the room!"

Sir Pigglesworth made a face. He wasn't sure he was going to like eating jewels for dinner.

When it was Sir's turn to order, he asked, "How do you recommend I have my sapphires cooked?"

After they ordered, Sir turned to JoAnn. "Is it really safe to eat jewels?" he asked. "Won't they give you a belly ache?"

JoAnn smiled. "They're pretty to look at, but they're not safe to eat."

Sir looked at Serena. Serena looked at Sir. Then they both looked at all the people eating sapphires at that moment, without knowing that it wasn't safe!

Suddenly they both jumped up on their chairs and began waving their arms.

"Everyone stop eating!" they screamed. "The food isn't safe! This lady said so!"

They pointed at JoAnn who looked completely shocked.

Everyone stopped eating and turned to stare at them.

"Really!" Sir insisted. "You should never eat jewels! It's not safe! This is the sapphire room and there are sapphires in your food!"

Everyone just laughed and went back to eating their dinner.

Sir Pigglesworth and Serena sat down, their cheeks turning bright red.

"Why is everyone laughing at us?" Sir Pigglesworth asked. JoAnn explained that there weren't any jewels in the food.

Sir and Serena slumped down in their chairs feeling embarrassed.

They quickly forgot to be embarrassed after they were brought all the food they could eat...which was a lot!

When they got back to their rooms, Serena and Sir had a surprise waiting for them on their beds.

The cabin steward had left them each a towel animal.

Sir Pigglesworth's animal was a platypus and Serena's was a rabbit.

They were so excited they both ran from their rooms with their new prized possessions and bumped right into one another in the hallway.

The towel animals flew out of their hands and landed in a heap on the floor. "I think we created a new animal," Sir Pigglesworth said.

"We can call it a platybbit," Serena said, and they both giggled.

Chapter 4

The next day in Camp Ocean, they were decorating Mexican sombreros. They had lots of fun covering their sombreros with colorful beads, bright ribbons, pom poms and construction paper.

When they finished their masterpieces, they held a parade around the pool with Sir Pigglesworth leading the way.

Sir Pigglesworth's hat was too big for his head and it slid down over his eyes. He couldn't see and he tripped.

He bumped right into a man who was holding a tray of soft drinks. The drinks splashed over everyone in the chairs.

Even though it was an accident, they weren't very happy.

Sir Pigglesworth pushed up his hat, apologized and ran away as fast as his hooves could go!

That night they had dinner at the Chef's Table in the galley. The galley is where food is prepared for the guests.

They were served lots of fancy foods that Serena and Sir had never heard of… and weren't sure they wanted to.

"Try a little bit of everything," the chef said. "I bet you'll like it.

Sir Pigglesworth made a face, but he reached one hoof out and slowly picked up a piece of escargot. Serena held her breath as he raised it to his mouth and opened wide.

At the last minute, he shoved it in Serena's mouth instead!

Serena started to protest, but suddenly her expression changed. "This is good!" she said, grabbing a piece and shoving it in Sir Pigglesworth's mouth.

The chef made an appearance at their table to see how they liked their meal.

Sir Pigglesworth patted his tummy and smiled. "You know," he said, "I didn't think I would like sea food. After all, it looks like snails and fish, but that was the best meal I have ever eaten."

"I'm glad," said the chef. "Why don't you and the rest of the guests join me on a tour of the galley?"

Sir Pigglesworth was so full he could barely walk, but he was too excited to say no.

He followed the chef, waddling the whole way.

Sir Pigglesworth and Serena were amazed by the huge dishwashers and the piles of dirty dishes. They also saw servers balancing heavy trays of food on one hand.

Sir Pigglesworth and Serena slipped away as the chef talked to the guests.

"I want to be a waitress," Serena said grabbing a tray and several plates of food. She stacked the tray full, just like she had seen the servers do minutes before.

"I'll be the dishwasher," Sir Pigglesworth said as the man loading dirty dishes stepped away from the sink.

Serena headed for the door to the dining room, while Sir Pigglesworth picked up the water hose that rinsed the dishes before they were loaded into the dishwasher.

Just then, one of the servers walked into the kitchen and ran straight into Serena. Her tray began to wobble as she lost her balance; she squealed in panic.

Sir Pigglesworth spun around while in the middle of rinsing a plate, and sprayed the server with hot water.

The server stepped to the side trying to avoid getting soaked and bumped into Serena again by accident.

She lost her balance and the plates flew off the tray across the room and slammed into the chef who had stepped forward to see what was happening.

Sir Pigglesworth and Serena panicked. They wanted to run, but they couldn't because they were too full from dinner.

Chapter 5

"I don't understand why we're in so much trouble," Serena said the next day as they arrived in Cozumel. "We both said we're sorry!"

"You're not in trouble," JoAnn said. "We just want to keep a very close eye on you. We don't want to have another mess to clean up."

"Besides, I think you'll have a lot of fun at the beach," JoAnn said as they walked through a long building.

Sir wasn't thinking about the fun he would have at the beach. He was having fun looking at all of the things in the building.

There were clothes, souvenirs, and a golden statue of a Mexican cowboy wearing a sombrero with a gun in his hand.

"He looks so real," Sir Pigglesworth said reaching out to touch the man's hand. It felt warm and soft.

"He feels so real," Serena said. Suddenly the man moved and Serena jumped back.

"He is real!" she cried. The man winked at them.

Sir Pigglesworth and Serena ran screaming out of the building and into a courtyard with lots of brightly decorated stores and restaurants.

Once outside, they calmed down and began to check out the donkey and cow chair statues around them.

They even had JoAnn take their picture with them–after they poked both to make sure they weren't alive.

As they walked a little further, they came to a poster of the Three Amigos with cutout circles where their heads should be.

"We have to get our pictures taken with our faces in them!" Sir Pigglesworth exclaimed jumping up and down excitedly.

"But there's only two of us, and there's three of them," Serena pointed out.

Sir gave Bill puppy dog eyes. When Bill agreed to be the third amigo, Sir Pigglesworth whispered to Serena, "that look works every time."

As soon as the picture was taken, Sir Pigglesworth was off and running again. He noticed a joker statue and he swung from it just like a monkey.

By the time they pulled Sir Pigglesworth away, JoAnn and Bill were exhausted. They decided to take a boat ride so they could rest a little bit.

They settled in on a glass bottom boat that took them past 7 Mile Beach. Through the glass, they saw fish, brightly colored coral, sea turtles, and lobsters.

Sir Pigglesworth and Serena were so fascinated that they pressed their faces tight to the glass so they wouldn't miss a thing!

When the boat let them off at the beach, Sir Pigglesworth and Serena headed straight for the jet skis.

They flew across the water.

"I bet we can go faster than you guys can!" Sir Pigglesworth called to Bill and JoAnn who were riding a jet ski next to them.

"Don't go any faster." JoAnn said. "It's too dangerous."

"Danger is my middle name!" Sir Pigglesworth laughed loudly.

"Your name is Sir Danger Pigglesworth?" Serena asked.

"Slow down!" Bill yelled to them, but Sir just sped up faster.

"Watch this!" Serena said as she stood up on the seat.

Once she was able to get her balance she struck a ballet pose.

She immediately lost her balance and fell backwards into the water.

Luckily, Bill and JoAnn were right there to scoop her up.

Sir Pigglesworth felt bad and slowed down while Bill put Serena safely back on her seat before they all headed back to the beach.

Chapter 6

That evening back on board the ship, they were in the dining room having a delicious dinner.

Sir Pigglesworth was still pouting about them cutting his jet skiing adventure short. He insisted that it wasn't his fault Serena had fallen off.

He was still upset when the servers began to sing and dance around the room, inviting all of the guests to join them.

Sir Pigglesworth couldn't resist dancing and singing. He flew from his seat and joined in the fun, forgetting all about being upset with his friends.

He was having a blast!

Soon Bill, JoAnn, and Serena joined in the fun, waving their napkins in the air.

After dinner, they went to the theater to see a show. The cruise director invited JoAnn up to the stage.

Sir Pigglesworth, refusing to be left out of the fun, jumped up onstage to join her.

"I see you have a little pink friend with you," Mike said to JoAnn.

JoAnn smiled. "This is Sir Pigglesworth," she told him.

"We have a royal pig with us," Mike exclaimed. "That's a first!"

"You have two royals, I'm Princess Serena." The little Princess jumped up onto the stage. The audience went wild with applause and laughter.

Soon they were all dancing to the YMCA song and having a great time!

Bright and early the next morning, everyone was wide awake and ready for another adventure in Cozumel.

"We need to catch a bus, " Serena said. "Let's hurry!"

They walked off the ship and soon they were on a bus riding to the Tulum ruins.

While they were walking up to the stone entrance of the ruins, their tour guide gave them a little history about the settlement.

"Tulum means wall, which refers to the wall around the ruins. It is sixteen feet tall and twenty-six feet thick."

"Because they didn't have any stores in those days, this is where they traded their goods in exchange for new items."

Sir Pigglesworth imagined what it must have been like to trade things instead of buying them.

He wondered what he could get if he traded one of his candy bars. He decided he would have traded one of Serena's candy bars instead.

During the tour, they saw a large round stone with pictures and symbols covering it. Their guide said this was an ancient Mayan calendar.

There was a 'DO NOT TOUCH' sign right next to it, but Sir Pigglesworth just couldn't resist.

When he touched the stone, it rocked back and forth and starting rolling! It hit the wall. Luckily the stone didn't break.

The group was asked to leave the ruins. They were upset at Sir Pigglesworth. He said he was sorry to everyone for causing trouble.

By now everyone was very hot and tired and wanted to go down to the beach.

"I'm sweating like a pig," Sir Pigglesworth said wiping his brow.

Serena rolled her eyes. "You are a pig," she reminded him.

"Then I'm sweating like a girl," Sir Pigglesworth said with a mischievous grin.

Serena pulled back her hand to punch him in the arm.

JoAnn grabbed her and led her down the staircase to the beach so they could all splash in the water and cool off their bodies…and their tempers.

Chapter 7

The next day, they took a ride on the Atlantis Submarine. It took them one hundred feet under the water. It went around a coral reef and through the marine park. It was very colorful.

Sir Pigglesworth was just a little jittery about being under the water. But he didn't want anyone to know so he tried to act 'cool' about it.

They spotted the wreck of an old pirate ship. Having seen a pirate ship before, Sir Pigglesworth recognized it right away!

When the ride was over, they headed back to the surface and picked up their 'dive certificates.'

Sir Pigglesworth and Serena were very proud.

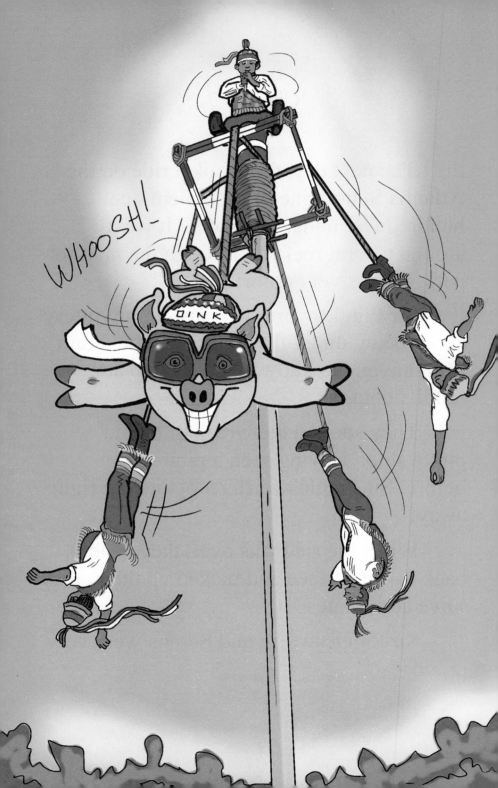

Just then something in the sky caught Sir Pigglesworth's eye. When he looked up, there were people flying upside down from a pole!

"I gotta try that!" Sir Pigglesworth exclaimed forgetting he was a little afraid of heights.

Before anyone could stop him he scampered up to the top of the pole. He grabbed hold of a rope, slipped it over his hoof and took off flying. He was having the time of his life!

When they were all lowered to the ground, Sir Pigglesworth found out that the pole flyers were part of an ancient Mayan ritual.

He was also very happy that he had gotten over his fear of heights!

He could just imagine all the exciting new adventures waiting for him!

Sir Pigglesworth hopped out of bed early the next morning. The captain had invited him and Serena to take a tour of the bridge.

There was a lot of action going on when they arrived with everyone doing their job to keep the ship sailing smoothly.

The Captain showed them the computers that helped to keep the ship on its course.

When he showed them the steering wheel, Sir Pigglesworth jumped up to hold on to it and accidentally turned the wheel.

The ship started zigzagging back and forth like crazy-eights!

The crew rushed around trying to straighten it out. When they were told it was time to leave the bridge, Sir Pigglesworth just couldn't understand what the commotion was all about.

Finally oday was JoAnn's birthday!

All through dinner with the Captain, Sir Pigglesworth anxiously waited for the moment when he could give his present to her.

Maybe…just maybe…she would share it with him.

After finishing dinner, their server brought out a big cake with lots of candles.

Sir Pigglesworth was so busy thinking about his present that he didn't see what was happening. He looked up and all he saw was fire!

He jumped on his chair and yelled "Fire!" In a panic, he threw his cup of water over the cake.

The 'fire' was out, but some of the water spilled on his chair and he slipped, falling into the cake.

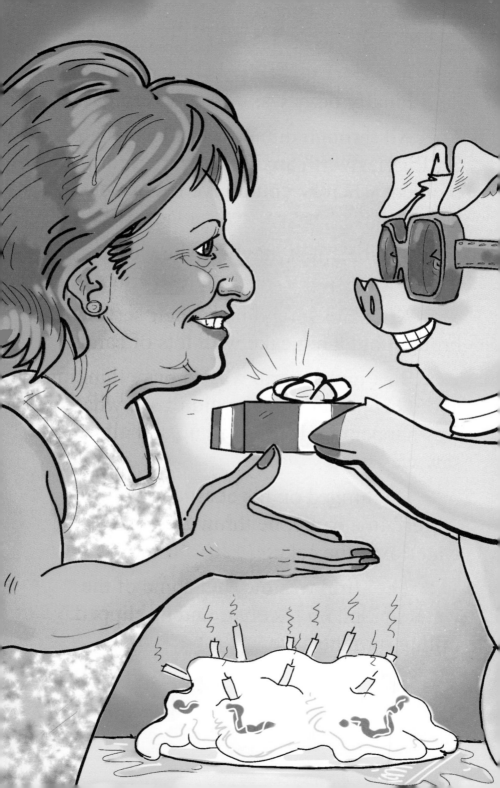

JoAnn and Bill pulled him out of the cake. Another one was brought out to the table, this time without candles.

Now it was time to open presents. Serena gave her a heart necklace. Bill gave her a diamond ring.

Finally it was Sir Pigglesworth's turn. He stood up and clinked his spoon on his glass. "I would like to give this present to my very dear friend, JoAnn."

He bowed low and handed her his gift.

She loved it! Just as he had hoped, she shared with everyone at the table.

Walking out of the restaurant, Sir Pigglesworth whispered in Bill's ear, "Don't worry. I'm sure JoAnn liked your ring."

"But next year I would get her candy. It was *clearly* her favorite present!"

The next day it was time to go home.

They took one last walk around the ship, remembering all the fun times they had together.

They asked someone to take their picture. Then it was time to say goodbye.

"I don't want to go home," Serena said as she hugged her friends.

"Oh, don't worry," Sir said. "We'll see them again soon." He leaned over and whispered, "after all, they're going to need us to teach them how to drive a jet ski."

"They must not know what they're doing if they drive that slow."

They parted ways, already excited about the next adventure they would share!

THE END

Places of interest

Carnival Breeze
http://bit.ly/29dTj7y

Atlantis Submarine
http://atlantissubmarines.travel/

Tulum Mayan Ruins
http://www.tulum.com/attractions/mayan-ruins

Mayan Pole Flyers
http://bit.ly/28W1XrI

Cozumel, Mexico
http://bit.ly/1Kv6WOj

Join us for Book 7
Sir Pigglesworth's Adventures in San Juan, PR.

For information on other "*Sir Pigglesworth Adventure Series*" books, please visit:
www.SirPigglesworth.com

Books available at
www.SirPigglesworth.com
www.BarnesandNoble.com
www.Amazon.com

Meet the Author:
www.JoAnnWagner.com
https://www.facebook.com/joann.g.wagner
Twitter: @AuthorJoJo

Bulk purchases available at:
www.SirPigglesworthPublishing.com

For free cartoons delivered daily to your email
visit: www.SharingSmilesAroundTheWorld.com